This Little Caterpillar's Name Is

_____

Pete The Caterpillar:
his transformational journey
Author: Jordan De La O

Illustrations by Anastasiia Khodak

Editing by Bianka Walter

Connect with the Author:
Facebook.Instagram.YouTube: **Jordan Diebel Delao**

www.jordandelao.com

Pete The Caterpillar
his transformational journey

written by: Jordan De La O

Illustrated by: Anastasiia Khodak

"I'll never be free. It's not for me,"
Pete says with his head hanging low.

A voice is heard in the distance,
with quite the thick Brooklyn accent.

"Whoa, whoa, whoa! What did I just hear?"
Pete looks around surprised and a little puzzled.

"Yes, you. Little greenie. Hey!
Snap outav' it kid. You ain't going nowhere
with that woe-is-me attitude."

"The name's Donny, but you can call me The Brooklyn Bug.
Grew up under the bridge with all my cousins.
Had to fight for survival just to get food.

Daily living was a real bug;weaving in and outta cars,
taxis beeping, fire trucks wailing, and don't get me started
with those pedestrians and tourists...eesh!

Rough tough life, ya know?"

"Wow...I'm just trying to get out of here," uttered Pete

The Brooklyn Bug counsels Pete by saying,
"Kid, I don't know much in life, but what I do know is
maybe it ain't your job to set yourself free.
Give it a little time.

My father once told me, 'Son, things of great value take time to achieve; there ain't no secret ingredient to it and you can always do better.

It's a hard life, but if you can remain patient in trials and keep moving forward, you can achieve anything you set your mind on.

Ignore the naysayer gnats, the moping mosquitoes, the fearful flies and the woe-is-me wasps. They ain't no good for ya'.

"Gee, thanks!" exclaimed Pete.

"Don't mention it kid. It's a bug-eat-bug world out there
and us bugsters gotta stick together, ya know?"
said The Brooklyn Bug.

And that is how Pete learned PATIENCE.

"Ugh, oh no, not again. Will I ever get out of this jar?"

Pete thought to himself.

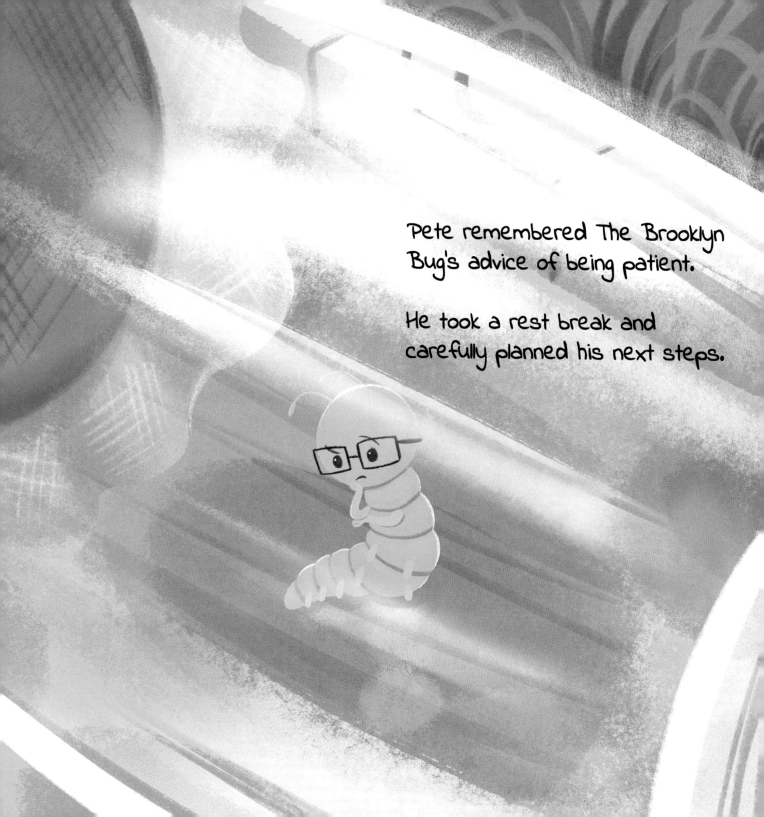

Pete remembered The Brooklyn Bug's advice of being patient.

He took a rest break and carefully planned his next steps.

Attempting to get out of the jar,
Pete took a deep breath.

"1....2...3...Ughhh...Aghhh...C'mon, Pete!
You've got this!"

Encouraging himself, "I can do this.
I am strong. I've got what it takes."

with one final attempt, Pete cried,
"Coming in strrrroooooonnnggggg!" BAM!!!

Pete's whole body banged against the
glass as he bounced back in exhaustion.
"Oh, man," thought Pete.

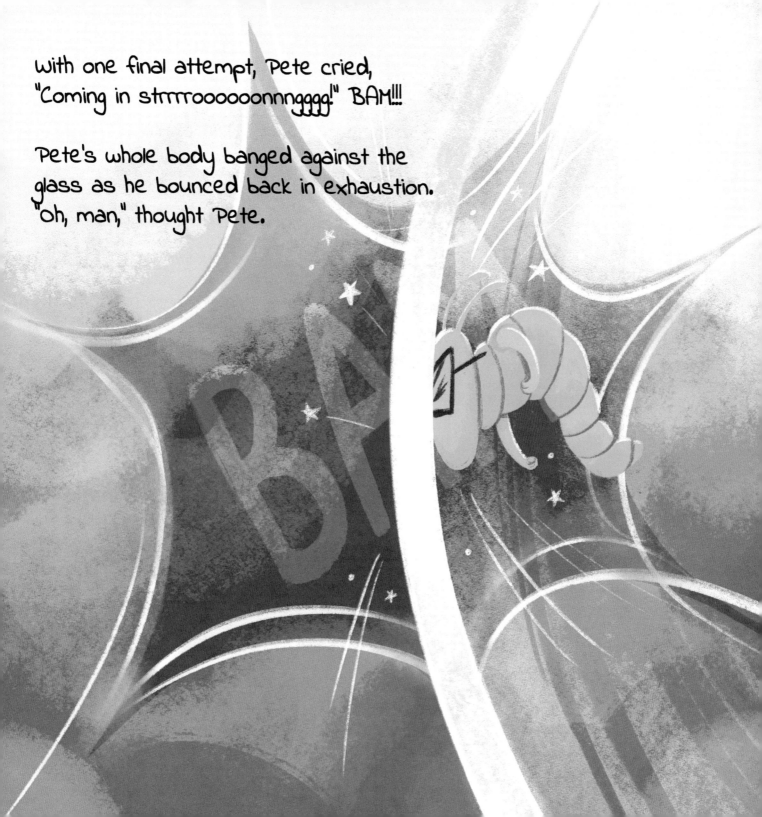

"Excuse me little bug, I don't mean to be rude, but I see you're having a little trouble," Evelyn politely whispers.

Embarrassed, Pete looks up cautiously. "oh, hi...I didn't see you there."

She responds, "oh, I'm sorry if I scared you. Let me introduce myself. My name is Evelyn, but you can call me Sweet Evie. What's your name?"

"Uhhhhhhh – I'm, I'm, I'm Pete. Uh, yes, I'm having some trouble.

The thing is, I've lived in this mason jar for my entire life and I'm getting too big for it.

I just want to get out and stretch my legs, ya know?

I don't know what to do anymore." Pete sighs.

"May I offer you some advice?"
Sweet Evie asks.

"Yes please!" Pete eagerly responds.

"Okay." Sweet Evie starts to explain, "Let me tell you about a time when I was struggling just like you and how someone helped me.

It was a rainy afternoon at my grandma GiGi's home. My brother, Preston and I were sooo bored, so we gathered an old puzzle from her attic.

Not too long after playing, I became quite annoyed with this one particular puzzle piece.

I tried and tried to squish it here and squish it there and wiggle it here and wiggle it there, but it would not fit anywhere!

Preston, my dear baby brother, tried to help, but I pushed him away! Out of my frustration, of course.

Feeling angry and confused, I let out a 'not so sweet' kind of cry.

Grandma GiGi came rushing in to my rescue, lifted my head up and told me, 'It's going to be alright, we'll figure this out together.'

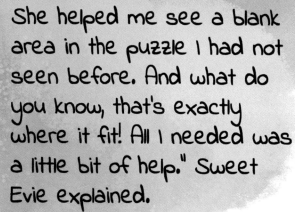

She helped me see a blank area in the puzzle I had not seen before. And what do you know, that's exactly where it fit! All I needed was a little bit of help." Sweet Evie explained.

"Hmmm," Pete said with confusion. "I'm not following."

Sweet Evie politely explained, "Basically, Pete, I'm your 'Grandma GiGi' here to help set you free from something you can't see.

You've been working hard on your own to get out of this jar, but you need a little bit of help, and I'm your helper!

All you have to do is ask."

"ohhhh...okay, let's do this!
will you please help me out of here?"
Pete asked with expectancy!

With Pete's eagerness,
Sweet Evie kneeled down
in the grass beside Pete.
She rotated the jar away
from the trash can and
bench ever so subtly.

She placed her fingers
on the canning ring and
with just a couple of
twists, unscrewed it.

"Be free little buddy!" Sweet Evie exuded with joy.

Astonished, Pete closed his eyes and took
in the crisp breeze swirling in and out of the jar.

"Oh! The freedom," thought Pete.

Pete inched his way out of the jar and felt the moist grass on his itty bitty feet for the first time.

"Wow! This is pretty cool! Thank you Sweet Evie!" Pete said with joy.

"You're most welcome Pete. Happy to help!" Sweet Evie responded.

And that's how Pete realized when you get stuck in a difficult situation, sometimes we need to ask for a little bit of HELP.

A few months passed by and even though Pete was enjoying his life outside the jar, he sensed a bigger purpose and change was to come.

He felt the need to move to a quiet place, somewhere he could feel safe and prepare for his new transformation. Pete ventured off to a nearby oak tree.

He inched his way up the bark and along his path, was met by an old wise British owl who stopped him in his tracks.

"Hoo Hoo Hoo, Hoo do we have here?"
the old wise owl asked.

"Hi, sir. I'm Pete. Excuse me, but I need to
inch past you to-"

"Don't be silly. I know Hoo you are.
I spotted you a mile away. My name is
Sir Gerald. I know why you're here,"
Sir Gerald declared.

"You do?" Pete asked surprisingly.

"Why, yes." Sir Gerald responded.
"You're not the first and you won't be the last. I've lived life a little longer than you to observe a thing or two.

They don't call me the 'old wise owl' for nothing!

AnyHOO, I can help you through this transformational journey," Sir Gerald said.

"Okay...I'm listening..." Pete said with hesitation.

Mmm Hmm." Sir Gerald cleared his throat.

"You see, young chap, you are about to transform from your child life to your adult life. In order for you to mature into Hoo you are meant to be, you must go through a process called metamorphosis.

"Meta-whaaaat?" Pete interrupted.

"Hold on, let me explain." Sir Gerald said. "Metamorphosis simply means transformation from immature to mature.

You see, you will shed the old layers of your skin and form a hard shell that covers your body, called a chrysalis.

Inside this chrysalis, you will grow more than you can ever imagine!

Now, I must warn you young chap, this will be an uncomfortable time, but you have to remain positive. Keeping a positive outlook will get you through this hard time.

Once you're mentally and physically mature, you will break free from the chrysalis and emerge into Hoo you are destined to be!

oh young chap, what a sight that will be to see!"
Sir Gerald said cheerfully.

"Thank you, Sir Gerald. I believe my time has come and I must begin this meta-process you speak of," said Pete.

"Yes, go right ahead young chap. I'm here for you,"
Sir Gerald said with comfort.

"Thank you, Sir Gerald. I will remain positive. See you soon."
Pete nods.

And that's how Pete learned that you need to remain
POSITIVE when you are going through a change in your life.

Two weeks passed by and the time finally came
for Pete to embrace his new transformation!

Amazed of everything he was able to accomplish, Pete took a moment to admire his new beautiful wings.
"Wow! I can't believe all this time I was meant to be a butterfly!" Pete exuded with joy.

HELP

PATIENCE

POSITIVITY

Knowing that his maturity was now complete,
he nervously looked down at the world below,
collected his thoughts, closed his eyes,
released a deep breath, and courageously
leaped into the open air!

The excitement and anticipation was too much for the old wise owl to just sit there, so Sir Gerald sprung off the branch and caught up with Pete in midair.

"I am so proud of you! You remained **positive** during the hard times and now look at you go, mate!" Sir Gerald cheered him on as they flew in sync.

"Thank you for helping me on my transformational journey!
I couldn't have done it without you all!" exclaimed Pete with
exuberant joy.

A message from Pete:
"Listen up children...to grow your wings and be transformed into the beautiful butterfly YOU are meant to be, you must remember that it takes PATIENCE, a little bit of HELP, and POSITIVITY."

About the Author

Jordan is a carefree, sunny-side-up, up and coming author who has cared for many children throughout her young adult life as a nanny. Her passions reside in the performing arts of dancing, singing & acting. When she is not performing on stage or enjoying the great outdoors, she is snuggled up with her  hubby and kitty while filling her mind with inspirational books & movies. She believes ALL young caterpillars have been called to a greater purpose, just like Pete. She resides in the Dallas-Fort Worth Metroplex.

About the Illustrator

Anastasiia is an illustrator and digital artist based in Ukraine. She has worked on several projects and can design portraits of your friends, loved ones, or your furry friends! She can definitely bring your story to life in a fun creative way!

Jordan's reason for writing the book

On January 3, 2021, the Lord woke up Jordan early in the morning with the repetitive words of "The Brooklyn Bug" and "Snap outav' it, kid". Half asleep and somewhat perplexed, lying in bed, she wrote the first chapter of *Pete The Caterpillar* on her iPhone in 30 minutes. Several months later, she revisited her story and decided to follow through by writing her first children's book.

The story of *Pete The Caterpillar* is a comparable journey of how Jordan has been undergoing her own transformational "Life Cycle of a Butterfly." She is maturing and developing her own wings of beauty while soaring into her God-designed destiny!

Jordan hopes that everyone reading this book will grab hold of a lesson no matter what season of life you are in. We can all learn patience, help, and positivity at some point in our lives.

She dedicates this book to all the young caterpillars who are undergoing their own transformational journey. Everyone develops their wings on their uniquely given time. No one person's journey is the same. May we all learn a thing or two from Pete's journey.

Quote from the author

"The main reason for developing the character Pete was because I felt like I could relate to him through the different stages of his life as a caterpillar. I had struggled for many years feeling lost, confused and wandering through life aimlessly not having a sense of purpose and direction. Like Pete, I was stuck in a jar, figuratively speaking! It has taken many years of self discovery, crying and praying on my bedroom floor to my daddy God in those hard times. I inched my way each year and learned valuable lessons that kept me moving forward. I thank the Lord Jesus for all his guidance and for the many individuals who helped steer me along my path. As you have read in my book, Pete had the help of his friends. We are not alone in this process. Your individual journey is uniquely crafted just for you. No need to compare. Fight the good fight, don't give up, reach out for help because one day, you will soar to new heights!"

-Jordan De La O

As I reflect on my writing, I want to share a little insight with you.

My inspiration for Sir Gerald came to me because I see him like my daddy God. He knows our thoughts, struggles, and our destiny. He is and will always be right beside us. At the end of the story, Sir Gerald flew side by side with Pete. God will fly side by side with you too, if you allow him.

> "The Lord himself goes before you and will be with you; he will never leave you nor forsake you. Do not be afraid; do not be discouraged." -Deuteronomy 31: 8 NIV

Thank You

- To the good **Lord** for imparting the desire to create, inspire, and for putting up with all my caterpillar years.

- To my **husband, Aaron**, for always having a listening ear, your continual motivation, and your encouragement to pursue my dreams! You've taught me to persevere and to keep moving forward. This book became a reality because of your helping hand and your generous love! I love you "Bubby Bear!"

- To my **mom, Marcia** who inspired me for Grandma GiGi. You've supported my talents and volunteered for almost every show I've done. 😄 Thank you for your gentle kindness during those lonely caterpillar years. I still remember that social butterfly pillow you gave me on that somber day and said, "Honey, one day you will have many friends."

- To my **dad, Gary**, who tells everyone, "She learned everything from me." I think we all know the real truth. 😉 Thank you for your support. Love you, Dad!

- To my **siblings, Jessica and John,** thank you for expressing and showing your love for all my creative ventures.

- To my **niece, Sweet Evie and my nephew, Preston,** for the inspiration of the characters in this book. One day soon you will be able to read this book on your own, my little caterpillars! Your aunt JoJo loves you more than you know.

- To **Big David De La O** who inspired me for The Brooklyn Bug. I admire how you don't take anything from anyone, you have a rough tough mental state, you tell it like it is, and you remind us that "you can always do better."

- To my **in-laws:** Thank you for the continued encouragement, prayers and love.

- To **Elizabeth De Moraes** for your guidance and coaching.

- To all the **young caterpillars** out there: keep on inching forward. You will grow your wings in due time!